My father sometimes calls our house a wildlife preserve. He says he never heard the pitter-patter of little feet the way people are supposed to when they have children. All he heard were wild whoops and thundering hooves. I guess the house *was* quieter before I came along. . . .

I told my Sunday school teacher about how I get into trouble for having a big, booming voice. Then I told her about wishing I could be Julie, because Julie does everything so neatly and never gets in trouble. But Miss Jenkins told me something nice about you, God. She said you love me just the way I am, but that you also love the way I can be. She said it takes work to be better people, but you've promised to help us. That's good. . . .

Elspeth Campbell Murphy

MARY JO BENNETT

Illustrated by Tony Kenyon

WISE
OWL

A Wise Owl Book
Published by Chariot Books, an imprint of David C. Cook Publishing Co.
David C. Cook Publishing Co., Elgin, Illinois 60120
David C. Cook Publishing Co., Weston, Ontario

MARY JO BENNETT
© 1985 by Elspeth Campbell Murphy

Illustrated by Tony Kenyon
Cover and book design by Catherine Hesz

Printed in the United States of America
90   5 4

Library of Congress Cataloging in Publication Data

Murphy, Elspeth Campbell.
  Mary Jo Bennett.

  Summary: Mary Jo tries very hard to behave well at school so she can go on a trip with her grandparents, but nothing seems to go right.
  [1. Schools—Fiction. 2. Behavior—Fiction]
I. Kenyon, Tony, ill. II. Title.
PZ7.M95316Mar   1985   [E]   85-17059
ISBN 0-89191-711-X

For the Hice family
with love

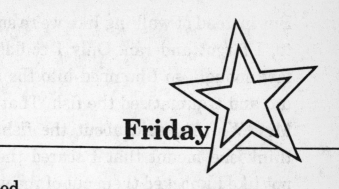

Friday

Dear God,

I guess this is a good time to start my prayer journal, because I'm in trouble again. Miss Jenkins, my Sunday school teacher, told us that you care about our troubles, God, and you want to help us, so I guess it's OK just to come right out and tell you.

Besides, if I waited for a time when I wasn't in trouble, I might not ever write anything at all!

So here's what happened. Mrs. Whitney, my regular-school teacher, said I could sharpen my pencil in school this morning.

7

But instead of walking like we're supposed to, I forgot and ran. Only I couldn't stop fast enough, so I bumped into the aquarium and traumatized the fish. That's what Mrs. Whitney said about the fish, and I think she meant that I scared them. It's not like I knocked them out of the water or anything.

But Mrs. Whitney was still pretty upset about it, and she told me I would have to sit on the wood at recess.

Sitting on the wood is this rule Mrs. Whitney and the other teachers have for recess. There's this little wooden bench along the edge of the playground. And when kids are being punished with no recess, they have to sit on the wood until the teacher tells them they can get up and play.

I hate sitting on the wood. Next to stay-

ing after school for detention, it's the worst thing. That's because it makes my legs itchy to watch all the other kids running and swinging and climbing on the monkey bars when I have to sit there. And when that dumb Vanessa heard what Mrs. Whitney said about me having to sit on the wood, she leaned over and whispered, "Ha—ha for you, Mary Jo." Only she didn't say it loud enough for Mrs. Whitney to hear.

Vanessa made me so mad I leaned over and scribbled on her paper—which probably wasn't a smart thing to do, when you think about it, because right away Vanessa yelled, "Mrs. Whitney! Mary Jo *ruined* my paper!" And that wasn't even really the truth, because it was only a little pencil mark. Still, it made Mrs. Whitney madder at me. She made me

10

switch desks with another kid so that Vanessa and I don't have to sit anywhere near each other. I'm glad about that. But I wasn't glad when Mrs. Whitney told me she was going to write a note to my parents.

● ● ●

Mrs. Whitney isn't a mean teacher. In fact, I think she's nice most of the time, but she doesn't like it when kids break the rules or act too wild or don't cooperate and get along.

So when the class had free time, Mrs. Whitney called me up to her desk to talk to me privately.

She said she always gave kids some time at the beginning of the year to get used to her and to being in a new, harder grade. But she said I should have settled down by now and that she wants to see some changes in the way I act. She said, "Mary Jo, I know it's hard for you to sit still, because you're very active. And it's hard for you to keep the noise level under control, because you have a very big voice for someone your size."

I told her I knew the rules but that I sometimes just forgot them and that I didn't mean to be bad. She said I would have to try harder to behave. She wrote a note to my parents and told me she would like them to send an answer back on Monday morning.

● ● ●

Vanessa saw Mrs. Whitney give me the note, and on the way out of school she said in this phony, icky-sweet voice, "Don't forget to give your parents the note from Mrs. Whitney. You *know* how you forget things. Just a friendly reminder."

12

I wanted to run after her and pull her hair or something, but my friend Julie said it would only make things worse. Julie never gets in trouble, but she is still nice. Vanessa never gets in trouble, either, but she is a snot.

Julie had to go to the dentist right after school, so I thought I would have to walk home alone. But then I got a nice surprise. I saw my father coming down the sidewalk. He was pushing my brother, Matthew, in the stroller. Matthew isn't even one yet. And our big dog, Bruno, was kind of bouncing along beside. Even Mr. Ferguson decided to come along for the walk, only he wasn't walking. He was riding with Matthew in the stroller.

I just realized how funny that would sound if somebody besides you or me read this journal, God. (Which they can never do, because it's private between you and me, right?) Somebody else wouldn't know that Mr. Ferguson is a cat!

My father likes to go for walks so he can think about his sermons. One time a funny thing happened. He and I were out walking, and we met this older kid who goes to our church. And my father said hello to him. But the kid looked at us like he didn't know who we were, because he's just used to seeing Daddy in the pulpit at Apple Street Church. But then the kid said, "I didn't recognize you at first, Pastor Bennett. I didn't know you walked around loose like other people."

And even the kid realized how dumb that sounded, because he turned bright red. But my father just thought it was funny. And now whenever my father goes for a walk he says to my mother, "Margaret, I believe I'll walk around loose for a while." When my father thinks something is funny, he says it a lot.

I guess I should have shown my father the note right away, but I didn't want to ruin his nice walk.

It would have been different if it were my mother who came to get me. That's because sometimes I think she has X-ray vision or something. She would probably have seen the note right through my notebook. She could probably have read it without even opening the envelope.

But my mother has a church meeting on Friday afternoons, so I decided to save the note till later.

● ● ●

This is later. I'm out in the backyard with Bruno, and the note from Mrs. Whitney is in my pocket.

My mother just got home and started cooking dinner. She always says people should be relaxed when they eat, so they can digest their food properly—which is why I haven't shown them the note yet. I think my parents should relax and have a nice dinner. That makes sense, doesn't it?

Bruno is running and jumping and playing in the leaves and being goofy like always. But that's OK for him. Bruno doesn't understand life, because he's just a dog. He doesn't get notes from the teacher. Except if Bruno went to obedience school, he sure would get notes about his behavior.

My father likes to pretend that he doesn't know Bruno is a dog. He always says to my mother about Bruno and me, "Margaret, those two children shouldn't be allowed to play together. They set each other off." And he's always telling Bruno to wash the car and asking him if he knows his spelling words.

Sometimes people say that Bruno is as big as a horse. I wish Bruno could really be a horse. It's not that I don't want to keep Bruno as a dog, but you can't ride a dog no matter how small you are—and I'm the littlest one in my class. So that's why I need a horse.

I would keep Bruno as a dog and Mr. Ferguson as a cat, but I would like to have a horse, too.

Every year at Christmas I ask for a horse. And every year on my birthday I ask for a horse. My mother and father tell me I will *never* get a horse, because you can't have a horse where we live. But every year at Christmas and on my birthday I ask for a horse—*just in case.*

17

If I had a horse now, I would go galloping off to a faraway place where there are no such things as school and kids who get you in trouble and notes from the teacher.

● ● ●

Well, God, I showed my parents the note from Mrs. Whitney. I was going to save it till after supper, but somehow my mother guessed that there was something I needed to tell them. I don't know how she knew.

They were pretty upset. They said that Mrs. Whitney was absolutely right—that I need to stop goofing around and behave myself.

I told my parents that I was really sorry and that I really knew how to act better but that I just kept forgetting. And I promised I would settle down.

Then my father said, "Fine. Now I'll tell you what's going to happen.

18

"If you don't prove you can keep your promise to act better in school, something bad will happen to you—you'll be grounded for a whole week and not allowed to ride your bike."

That was *bad news*, God, because I think I would go crazy if I couldn't ride my bike.

I like to pretend that my bike is a horse that I can ride and ride and ride. I even gave her the name that I would give my horse if I get one—*Silver Lightning*.

But then my father said, "If you *do* keep your promise and prove that you can act better, then something good will happen to you." I was almost afraid to ask what, because sometimes people in trouble shouldn't push their luck by asking what rewards they're going to get.

But my father told me about it anyway, and I'm telling you, God, it was *so* good I

19

jumped up and clapped my hands and twirled around the kitchen.

Right away my parents reminded me that it wasn't a sure thing—that I had to *earn* it by being better in school.

Here's what it is. My Grandma and Grandpa Bennett are going to the country next weekend, and they want to take me with them. I'll be the only kid around—no cousins and not even Matthew. But the *best* part, the really superduper part, is that my grandparents will be visiting these friends who have a HORSE! *And they said I could ride her!!*

I have never gotten to ride a horse except for when I was little and rode the ponies that go around and around in a circle at the fair; I'm not even sure that counts.

I was so excited my father reminded me

20

again that it wasn't a sure thing. He said I have all this next week to prove to them and Mrs. Whitney that I can act right and cooperate. He said he would write to Mrs. Whitney on Monday and tell her the plan. Then on Friday they will decide together if I can go.

So, do you think maybe you could help me, God? I really would like to do a good job this week—not *just* because I want to go on the trip. I really want Mrs. Whitney and my mother and father to be proud of me, too.

● ● ●

I was just looking through our kitchen junk drawer, because sometimes I find stuff I can use. And way in the back I found half a box of those little stars you lick and stick on your paper. My mother said they were left over from when she

21

taught vacation Bible school and that I could have them if I wanted them.

The stars were really a useful thing to find. You know why? Because from now on whenever I do something good, I will give myself a star. I'll stick them right here in my journal.

I guess that is all for now, God.

Love,

Mary Jo

Saturday

Dear God,

Julie came over today, and when Mr. Ferguson saw her, he ran away and jumped up on the bookcase. This really bothered Julie, because she is crazy about cats and she wanted to play with him.

But that's the funny thing about Mr. Ferguson. He doesn't go to people who want him. Some people are allergic to cats, and some people are even afraid of cats—and *those* are the people Mr. Ferguson goes to. He likes to curl up on their laps and drive them crazy. So when that happens, one of us has to grab him right away and shut him up in the bedroom, which doesn't please him one little bit. He never wants to cooperate, and he *always* wants to have his own way.

It's funny to think that Mr. Ferguson is older than I am. My parents got him before I was born. They bought him from these people whose last name was Ferguson.

The people had already named him Fluffy, and that's what my parents were going to call him, too. But he was so dignified even when he was a kitten, that my parents started calling him Mr. Ferguson. So his real name is Mr. Fluffy Ferguson. But then you have to add our last name, too. I think it sounds nice when people have hyphens in their names, so his real name is Mr. Fluffy Ferguson-Bennett. I guess Bruno's name is plain old Bruno Bennett.

24

Anyway, it's funny to think of people and even cats being around before I was. Miss Jenkins told us in Sunday school that you have just always been here, God, and that you always will be. I like to think about that sometimes, even though I don't understand it.

● ● ●

Julie was so annoyed that Mr. Ferguson wouldn't play with her that she went home to get her own cat and brought him back here. Julie has a little kitten named Oreo. She named him that because he is black on both ends and white in the middle—like an Oreo cookie.

Bruno was outside, so he couldn't bother Oreo, and we figured Mr. Ferguson would just ignore any kittens who happened to be visiting. But instead Mr. Ferguson got jealous, and he tried to get us to stop pay-

25

ing attention to Oreo and start paying attention to him.

I told Mr. Ferguson that he was a silly old cat and that being jealous was dumb.

But then Julie said something that really surprised me, God! She said she thought Vanessa was jealous of me!

I asked her why. She said, "Because Vanessa doesn't like being the biggest one in the class. She would rather be little like you. And she can't run and climb the way you do. No one can, except maybe Curtis, but boys don't count for this. And you're the prettiest girl in the class, and everybody always notices you. You get lots of attention."

I said I didn't know about that, because I think the only attention I get is when I'm in trouble.

Then we started talking about who we

liked and who we didn't like in our class. Of course, I said I didn't like Vanessa. Julie didn't want to say she *doesn't* like Vanessa even though she doesn't exactly *like* her, either. But then Vanessa is *nice* to Julie.

When it was time for Julie to leave, I got my bike and walked her home. We put an old towel in the basket and tried to get Oreo to ride along, but he wanted Julie to carry him. That's the way Matthew is sometimes. He just wants to be held. I guess all babies are alike—even cat babies.

After Julie went in, I rode around for a while and thought about what she'd said about Vanessa. I couldn't figure it all out.

But just being on my bike reminded me that I'd better not fight with Vanessa, or Mrs. Whitney would tell my parents I

27

wasn't behaving—and then I would be grounded. No trip. No horse. No bike.

● ● ●

When I got home, I decided that I'd better practice being quiet and sitting still. And I thought up a good way to do that. I pretended to be a statue, because statues can't talk or move.

Pretty soon I got tired of standing there, so I decided there was no reason I couldn't sit down. In fact, it was even better, because we sit down so much in school.

While I was sitting there, Matthew crawled over to my chair, and my mother called to me from the kitchen to keep an eye on him.

It was hard not to bend down and pick him up and cuddle him, but I figured a statue couldn't do that. But Matthew didn't mind. What he really wanted was to

28

play with the Velcro on my gym shoes. It felt funny when he pulled the tabs up and down, but I sat really still anyway. I sat so still, Mr. Ferguson must have thought I was a piece of furniture, because he came and sat on my shoulder and put his paws on my head.

I suppose I looked pretty funny with Matthew playing with my feet and Mr. Ferguson playing with my head. At least my father thought so. He stopped as he was passing through the living room on his way out and asked what was going on.

I wasn't going to answer, because statues can't talk. But he didn't know he wasn't supposed to talk to me, so I figured it would be all right to answer this time.

"I'm a statue," I said, trying not to move my lips too much. "I'm practicing sitting and not talking."

30

My father just shook his head like he didn't understand me and promised to shoo all the pigeons out of the house so they wouldn't land on me. But of course we don't have any pigeons in our house in the first place.

When I first started pretending I was a statue I checked the clock. Then when I figured I had been sitting that way for half an hour, I cheated and turned my head a little bit to see what time it was. But only five minutes had gone by. I thought maybe the clock was broken.

I was still sitting there when the doorbell rang. People from church stop by our house a lot. I almost jumped up to answer the door, but just in time I remembered that I was a statue who couldn't move.

Bruno came charging through the room,

31

barking his fool head off, the way he always does when someone comes to the door.

Then my mother came running, wiping the flour off her hands on a kitchen towel. It was one of the ladies from our church at the door. She was scared to death of Bruno, because she didn't know him well enough to know how silly he was and that he just liked to hear himself bark to prove to us how brave he was. I don't know how much protection he would be against burglars, but Daddy says the ladies from the missionary society had better never get the idea to rob us.

My mother was trying to wipe her hands and hold open the door and shush Bruno and be nice to the lady all at the same time.

When she saw me being a statue she

said, "Mary Jo, why didn't you answer the door? Why on earth are you sitting there with that cat on your head?"

I started to explain about practicing being quiet, but my mother just gave me one of her we'll-talk-about-this-later looks and said to the lady, "Mary Jo will put Bruno in the bedroom. Would you like some coffee?"

● ● ●

Later I explained to my mother why I didn't move when the doorbell rang and why I didn't grab Bruno right away.

Mom said it was fine for me to practice behaving, but that it wasn't good behavior for me just to sit there when I was needed.

Well, God, this is the first time I've *ever* gotten in trouble for just sitting still and being quiet.

Life is hard to figure out sometimes. I

33

think I will give myself a star, because I tried to do something good. But I won't give myself two stars, since it didn't turn out right.

Love,
Mary Jo

Sunday

Dear God,

I got to Sunday school early the way I usually do, so I helped Miss Jenkins unpack her teaching stuff and pass out the Sunday school workbooks.

Then she said I could print the kids' names on the new memory verses chart. So at the top I put Apple Street Church, Room 10, in my super-best printing. Then I printed the names in A-B-C order: Curtis Anderson, Mary Jo Bennett, Julie Chang, Becky Garcia, Philip McConnell (who everybody calls Pug, but I thought I should put Philip on the chart), and Danny

Petrowski. The kids in my Sunday school class are all in my school class, too.

Julie Chang is my best friend. Sometimes I wish I could be Julie instead of me. She always gets her work done at school, and she gets picked for a lot of things because she's so responsible. Julie doesn't get upset or mad. She's nice to people, and everybody likes her and wants to be her friend.

Becky Garcia is really quiet and shy. She just moved here when school started, so I don't know her too well yet. Except I know she likes to read a lot. You wouldn't think anyone so quiet would ever get in trouble, but one time when Becky was supposed to be doing her math, she had a library book on her lap and was reading it. Mrs. Whitney got pretty upset then. And Becky looked like she was going to cry.

Nobody likes to get yelled at, but Becky especially doesn't like it.

Miss Jenkins never yells, but maybe she would have to if she had a big class of kids every day in regular school. Anyway, I like having Miss Jenkins for a Sunday school teacher. She always listens seriously when we talk to her or ask her about something. She sure knows a lot about you, God! But she says it's too much for anyone to understand absolutely everything about you.

Miss Jenkins is the one who gave our class notebooks so we could keep prayer journals. I told her I started mine, and she looked really pleased.

I told her that I probably wouldn't be there next Sunday, because I would probably be going on a trip with my grandparents where I would get to ride a horse.

Miss Jenkins remembered that I like

37

horses, and she said that was good news. Then she said, "Why do you say *probably*? Don't you know for sure if you're going?"

So I explained to her about Mrs. Whitney and the agreement. And Miss Jenkins said she was sure I could do it. That was nice of her to say so.

Then I told her about wishing I could be Julie, because Julie does everything so neatly and never gets in trouble. And even if people were jealous of her, they still wouldn't be snotty to her.

I told her nobody but me gets in trouble for having a big, booming voice and running into fish.

Then Miss Jenkins told me something nice about you, God. She said you don't want me to be anyone but Mary Jo. She says you love me just the way I am, but that you also love the way I *can* be. She says you want me to be a better Mary Jo, just like you want her to be a better Emily Jenkins.

Miss Jenkins says it takes work to be better people, but that you have promised to help us. That's good.

● ● ●

Today in church when Daddy told everybody to pray silently for a minute, I asked you to help me be good, God.

I suppose you already know this, but other times when Daddy had those silent minutes, I haven't prayed. Other times I just kept my eyes closed except for a tiny slit, and I looked around while I pretended to have my eyes closed all the way. But I don't think I will do that anymore. I think I will keep praying to you the way I did this morning. I bet you are glad to hear that, aren't you? And I will keep you posted about how I'm behaving.

Love,
Mary Jo

Monday

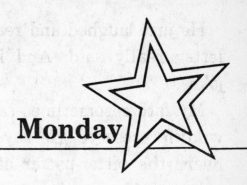

Dear God,

This morning at breakfast my father wrote a note for me to take to Mrs. Whitney that explained our agreement about the horse and everything.

I asked him what he was writing exactly, and he said, "I'm just telling her the simple truth—that you were raised by wolves and we found you on a camping trip and let you come and live at our house."

I said, "Daddy, don't you *dare* say that! What if Mrs. Whitney *believes* you? She might not understand the way you joke around all the time."

41

He just laughed and read me what the letter really said. And it was OK—no jokes.

My father sometimes calls our house a wildlife preserve. He says that he never heard the pitter-patter of little feet the way people are supposed to when they have children. All he heard were wild whoops and thundering hooves. I guess the house *was* quieter before I came along. There were only my parents and Mr. Ferguson—and we all know he doesn't make much noise.

● ● ●

Julie and I walked to school together, and we talked about who might get to be T.A. today.

Mrs. Whitney has this thing where she chooses people to be the T.A., which is short for Teacher's Assistant. She even has

42

badges in little plastic holders with a pin on them that say, "I am the girl T.A." and "I am the boy T.A." At the beginning of every morning she chooses a girl and a boy to be the special helpers for the day, and they get to do a lot of neat stuff like feeding the fish and passing out papers and taking notes to the office or other teachers and leading the way to and from recess and lunch.

And another neat part of being the T.A. is that you get to pick someone to be your *own* helper. And that person gets to wear a badge that says, "I am the girl T.A.'s friend" or "I am the boy T.A.'s friend." The girl T.A. picks a girl, and the boy T.A. picks a boy. So it works out well. You can pick anyone you want, but Julie and I have an agreement that I will pick her and she will pick me.

Mrs. Whitney usually picks the T.A.s first thing in the morning. And that is a kind of tense time, because everyone's sitting there thinking, *"Ooo,* pick me! Pick me!" But not everyone can get picked, of course. And if Mrs. Whitney calls a name that isn't yours, you still can hope that the T.A. will pick you to be the T.A.'s friend. But your name still might not get called, and then the picking is all over. And you're disappointed, but at least you can relax. Besides, there's always tomorrow.

The problem is if Vanessa gets picked, because she has this stupid little notebook. I don't know if Mrs. Whitney knows about it. In fact, I don't think many of the other kids know about it. The front of Vanessa's notebook has this really cute picture of a little mouse sniffing a flower that is way bigger than he is. I don't know how anything so cute could be used to get people in trouble, but it is. Here's how it happens.

Vanessa likes to make lists about people. She writes down who she thinks are the good kids in our class and who she thinks are the bad ones. She writes lists of who she likes and who she doesn't like. She writes down who brings neat things for Show and Tell and who brings boring things.

Those lists are bad enough, but when Vanessa is T.A., she writes down people's names so she can tell on them.

● ● ●

When I got to school, I was really excited about the plan my parents and I had and about getting to ride a horse next weekend. So I charged up to Mrs. Whitney with my letter and said, "MRS. WHITNEY! GUESS WHAT!!"

Mrs. Whitney just smiled the way my mother sometimes does when she's getting a headache. Then she said, "I really want to hear all about it, Mary Jo, but let's use our indoor voices, OK?"

The bad part was that Vanessa was right behind me, and she heard what Mrs. Whitney said about indoor voices. And Vanessa said to this other kid loud enough for me to hear (but not loud enough for

Mrs. Whitney to hear), "Honestly! Indoor voices! Mary Jo doesn't know how to talk yet, and Mrs. Whitney has to teach her like she's in kindergarten or something."

All I can say is, it's a good thing Vanessa sits clear across the room from me now or she would get it, let me tell you.

● ● ●

Neither Julie nor I got picked for the girl T.A. But at least Vanessa didn't get picked, either. A girl called Elizabeth got picked for the girl T.A., and she picked a girl called Amy to be the girl T.A.'s friend.

Curtis Anderson got picked for the boy T.A., and he picked a boy named John to be the boy T.A.'s friend.

● ● ●

Well, God, congratulate me. This was a pretty good day. I forgot and talked when I wasn't supposed to a couple of times, but

47

Mrs. Whitney didn't yell at me—she just gave me one of her warning looks, and I remembered right away to be quiet.

I just realized that I didn't give myself a star for yesterday, and that was a pretty good day, too. So I will give myself two stars for today.

Love,
Mary Jo

Tuesday

Dear God,

This day started off good, because the best thing happened! Mrs. Whitney showed us this film about the west, and it had this part in it about wild ponies. It showed them running and running—a whole herd of them—running wild and free.

And I thought, I wish I could *be* a pinto pony. I wish I could run and run and run and go as fast as I want or make as much noise as I want. Pinto ponies never even heard of indoor voices. That's because they only have one kind of voice—outdoors.

49

And no one ever tells them what to do.

But if I couldn't *be* a pinto pony, I would like to ride one. I know they don't let people ride them, but I would be different. One of the ponies would like me and trust me. And he would let the other ones know that it was OK for me to be along, and we would gallop and gallop in the wide open spaces. It would sort of be like always having recess.

While I was thinking all of this, I didn't realize that I was kind of galloping along with the horses right while I was sitting there watching them. Mrs. Whitney told me to settle down and sit still and pay attention. But I was paying attention. And I didn't even *know* I wasn't sitting still.

But that's not all that got me in trouble. When it was time for recess, I tried to stand still in line, but I was galloping my

50

fingers like horses running. I didn't think about what I was doing, and I accidentally galloped my fingers over the back of the kid ahead of me in line. Right away he turned around and yelled, "Hey, quit it!"

Then he tried to kick me, but I jumped back just in time. Unfortunately, I bumped into the kid behind me, who yelled, "Hey, quit it!"

Then Mrs. Whitney pulled me out of line and told me I would have to sit on the wood.

While I was sitting there feeling awful, Vanessa walked by and I heard her say, "I'll play with you, Julie." That really made me mad, because she knows Julie and I usually play together at recess. I think Vanessa wants Julie to stop being friends with me and start being friends with her, instead.

Julie looked at me like she wasn't sure what to do. I guess Julie didn't want to be mean to Vanessa, but she didn't want to make me feel bad, either.

Finally Julie said to her, "Let's go play with those kids on the merry-go-round." Julie can usually think up good ways to handle problems. This way she was sort of playing with Vanessa, but it wasn't like they were best friends or anything.

Becky came and sat beside me on the wood. She gave me a little smile and said, "Hi." She had a library book zipped inside her jacket that she took out and started to read. I just watched the kids on the swings.

In a way, that's the hardest thing of all about sitting on the wood—watching the kids on the swings.

I started saying a poem I know, and I hardly realized I was saying it out loud.

"How do you like to go up in a swing,
Up in the air so blue?
Oh, I do think it the pleasantest thing
Ever a child can do!"

I knew there was more of it, and I was wishing I knew the rest of it when Becky looked up and said,

"Up in the air and over the wall,
Till I can see so wide,
Rivers and trees and cattle and all
Over the countryside—

Till I look down on the garden green;
Down on the roof so brown—
Up in the air I go flying again,
Up in the air and down!"

I was really surprised Becky knew that poem, because she didn't even go to school here last year, which was when I learned it. But Becky said it's a famous poem and that lots of people know it.

I asked her who made it up, and she said, "Robert Louis Stevenson," without even having to stop and think about it.

That's the funny thing about Becky. She is so quiet, but she knows all this stuff. But she isn't snotty about how much she knows. Maybe she doesn't realize that not everybody knows as much as she does.

If Vanessa knew who wrote that poem (which I bet she doesn't), she would be snotty about knowing it. She would say, *"Nyah, nyah, nyah*. Robert Louis Stevenson. So there!"

Mrs. Whitney overheard Becky and me saying the poem. I didn't even know she was standing near us. And she said, "Well, Becky and Mary Jo! I didn't know you girls liked poetry!"

I said I like it because in poems the words move. Then I realized that sounded funny, because I didn't mean the words moved across the page. I explained that when you *say* the words, it *sounds* like they're running or skipping or just floating along. Like, when you say, "Up in the air I go flying again, up in the air and down," it sounds as if you're swinging.

Mrs. Whitney smiled and said that whole poem made her feel as if she were on a swing. Sometimes I've seen grown-ups on swings, but I guess I never thought about Mrs. Whitney that way. Except—this boy I know, who had Mrs. Whitney last year, said she went down the slide at their class picnic. So who knows? Maybe Mrs. Whitney comes out to the playground after we go home and gets on the swings.

Then Mrs. Whitney saw Becky's book

and said very nicely but firmly, "Becky, there's a rule about not bringing books out on the playground. This is a time to get some exercise. Look at all this beautiful sunshine. Now, go run and play."

Becky looked like she didn't want to go run and play—but she pretty much had to, because Mrs. Whitney said so. Becky was probably hoping Mrs. Whitney would punish her for bringing the book out by making her sit on the wood.

But Becky gave Mrs. Whitney her book to hold, and she walked around the playground a little bit, trying to look like she was running and playing.

I wanted more than anything to get off the wood and run around. And Becky wanted more than anything to sit on the wood and read her book. Sometimes things don't make sense, do they, God?

57

Finally Mrs. Whitney told me I had been sitting there long enough and that I could get up and have some recess. I jumped up and went running toward the swings. And, sure enough, Vanessa saw me, and, sure enough, she said, "Mrs. Whitney, Mary Jo's off the wood!"

Then Mrs. Whitney told Vanessa not to worry about things that don't concern her. Ha, ha for you, Vanessa, I thought to myself.

By now Julie was on the swings, and she wasn't ready to get off yet. There weren't any empty ones, so I went and sat on a teeter-totter and waited for Julie or someone to come along and climb on the other side.

Well, someone came along, all right. Vanessa! She pushed down on her end and jumped on.

58

Well, I'm the smallest one in the class, and Vanessa is the biggest—so you know what happened! I went shooting straight up in the air. And Vanessa sat down hard and wouldn't let me down.

So I said, "Buster Brown, let me down," the way you're supposed to.

But Vanessa wouldn't play right, and she wouldn't get up. So I started screaming, "Mrs. Whitney! Mrs. Whitney!"

I guess I must have made a lot of noise, God, because Mrs. Whitney and two other teachers came running. And Mrs. Whitney said, "Who fell? Who fell?"

And I said, "No one fell, Mrs. Whitney, but Vanessa won't let me down."

Then Mrs. Whitney looked really mad. She said, "You two girls! Honestly! Why can't you get along? The way you were screaming, Mary Jo, I thought someone had fallen and cracked his head open!"

I don't know why grown-ups always think kids are going to crack their heads open, but I figured this wouldn't be a good time to ask about that.

One of the teachers held my end of the teeter-totter so I wouldn't fall down too fast, and Mrs. Whitney made Vanessa get up carefully. Then Mrs. Whitney blew her whistle for the other kids to line up. She held on to Vanessa and me, so I was on one side of her and Vanessa was on the other.

"Well, Mary Jo," Mrs. Whitney said. "I thought you were going to settle down. I had high hopes for you yesterday, but now I'm not so sure."

And that suddenly reminded me of the weekend and my grandparents and riding a horse. I swallowed hard so that I wouldn't start to cry.

Vanessa leaned around Mrs. Whitney's back and stuck her tongue out at me. But I just pretended I didn't see, and in a way I didn't even care.

● ● ●

I guess this is a no-star day, right, God? But maybe I should give myself a star just to cheer me up. Maybe tomorrow will be better. Maybe I can think of something special to do. I still have three days to earn my trip.

Love,
Mary Jo

Wednesday

Dear God,

Remember yesterday I said I wanted to think of something special to do? Well, I started making a list of all the things I could do to make Mrs. Whitney and my parents proud of me so I could go on the trip. But the trouble was, I tried writing my list at the same time I was supposed to be taking my spelling test. I lost my place in the test and ended up with only three of the words written down.

So Mrs. Whitney told me I would have to stay after school and that the teacher who had detention duty would give me my spelling test.

● ● ●

The teacher gave me the test, and I got all the words right except one, which was pretty good. But my detention time isn't up yet.

My mother wasn't too happy with me when I called to tell her I had to stay. And Mrs. Whitney wasn't too happy when I didn't do my spelling test when I was supposed to. I need to think of something special to make them proud of me.

Guess what, God! I just thought of something special I can do. It's almost time for me to go home. But I won't go home right away. I'll sneak back into my own classroom. Then I'll get out some rags and a bucket from under the sink, and I'll wash the board for Mrs. Whitney.

She'll be so surprised and happy tomorrow! And she won't know who did this nice thing for her. Then I'll tell her it was me. She will be proud of me for thinking of it, and she'll tell the whole class what a nice thing it was for me to do.

I think I'll give myself a star for thinking of this good idea. Then, after I wash the boards, I'll give myself another star for my good work.

 • • •

I'm writing this just before I go to bed, God. I didn't tell anyone about the boards, because I want it to be a surprise. For once I can't wait to get to school in the morning. I want to see the look on Mrs. Whitney's face when she sees the nice thing I did for her. I'm sure she'll call my parents and tell them I should be allowed to go on the trip this weekend. It's fun when everything works out so well.

Love,
Mary Jo

 **Thursday**

Dear God,

Remember yesterday how I said it was so much fun when everything works out?

Well . . . I thought when we came in this morning that Mrs. Whitney would be smiling and in a good mood because someone had washed her chalkboards. I thought she would say something cute like, "I see the little elves have been here." And I thought that when she found out it was me, she would make me the T.A.

But when we came in, she looked really upset. All the kids stopped talking and just looked at her, because they knew some-

68

thing was wrong. I thought someone must have done something *so bad* that it made Mrs. Whitney forget how glad she was about the boards.

But guess what, God. It turned out the *washed boards* was the thing Mrs. Whitney was mad about!

Mrs. Whitney started talking in the different way she does when she's upset. She said, "Boys and girls, something very serious has happened. Yesterday afternoon I went to a great deal of trouble to put some specific material on the chalkboards. But when I came in this morning, I found to my dismay that someone had wiped the boards clean. I questioned the janitorial staff, but they know nothing about it. I suspect it was one of the older students, and I mean to get to the bottom of this. It's this sort of thing that leads to vandalism.

69

So if you have any information, I suggest you tell me now."

She waited for people to raise their hands, but, of course, nobody did. Especially not me. I just wanted to throw up.

Mrs. Whitney said, "Very well. If anything occurs to you, you may tell me privately."

I was wondering what to do when Mrs. Whitney surprised me by picking me for the girl T.A. I didn't feel like being the T.A. I never thought I'd say that, but that's how I felt, God. I picked Becky for the girl T.A.'s friend, because Julie was absent. Pug was the boy T.A. and, of course, he picked Danny for the boy T.A.'s friend. I wished Julie were there, because she would probably have told me what I should do. But I guess I knew already without having Julie to tell me. Maybe you told me what to do, God.

Mrs. Whitney has this rule that says when we can come talk to her. We can't talk to her when she has a reading group, but if we are doing seat work and she is at her desk, then we can ask to talk to her privately. If she is busy, she will tell us another time when we can talk. But if she is not too busy, she will listen to us then.

I hoped Mrs. Whitney wouldn't be too

busy, because I wanted to get telling her about the boards over with.

Mrs. Whitney must have been able to tell just by looking at me that I had something important to say, so she said we could step out into the hall to talk in private.

As soon as I started to tell her that I had washed the boards, I burst out crying. I explained about wanting it to be a nice surprise, and then I started crying even more.

Mrs. Whitney was serious, but nice, and I was really glad about that. She said she believed me about not meaning to do something wrong, and she said I was brave for telling her. But she said she wanted me to understand the problems.

Problem 1: Kids aren't supposed to get into the cabinets under the sink.

Problem 2: I shouldn't have erased the boards without asking first.

Problem 3: Kids aren't supposed to be alone in the rooms after school.

She said that last part was so important she thought I'd better hear it from Mr. Harley, the principal.

She gave me a note to take to him. But first she had me blow my nose and rinse my face and get a drink of water.

● ● ●

I am writing this in the secretary's office, God. Her name is Mrs. Miller, and she keeps an eye on kids who are waiting to see the principal.

There are no other kids waiting besides me, but the principal is talking to a kid in the other office.

I keep wondering what that other kid did and whether it's worse than what I did.

I wonder if the principal will be so mad at him that his madness will get all used up before he gets to me or if there will be plenty of madness left over. I wonder if the other kid did something on purpose or by accident.

It wasn't an accident that I washed Mrs. Whitney's boards. I really meant to do it. But it was sort of an accident that it turned out all wrong. I mean, I didn't get in trouble because I *tried* to be bad. Sometimes life is very confusing, God.

● ● ●

Mr. Harley was OK, I guess. He didn't exactly yell, but he gave me a good talking to.

The worst part was walking back into the classroom again after I had been in the principal's office. One of the kids from my class had gone to the nurse's office and saw

74

me sitting in the principal's office. When that kid went back, she whispered to the other kids where I was. And I think they all guessed about the boards.

When I got back, all the kids stared at me, but I didn't want to look at anybody. Do you know how hard it is not to look at anybody when they're all looking at you? I wished I could just be invisible.

Then that stupid Vanessa raised her hand and said, "Mrs. Whitney, does Mary Jo still get to be T.A.?" And Mrs. Whitney sounded really annoyed and said, "Of course she does. There's nothing more to discuss."

It made me feel better when Mrs. Whitney acted like Vanessa shouldn't have asked that question about me.

● ● ●

I stayed after school again today, but

this time it wasn't because I did anything wrong. I stayed after to help Mrs. Whitney and Danny put up a bulletin board. Danny drew pictures of all kinds of pets, and we cut them out and pinned them around the edges. The letters at the top said *Our Pets* and in the middle of the board were some "A" stories about pets we have or that we would like to have. And the really good thing was that one of the stories was *mine!* I wrote about Bruno and Mr. Ferguson and about the horse I might get someday.

When Danny and I came out of school, we saw my mother coming to meet me with Matthew and Bruno and Mr. Ferguson.

Danny was so proud of his pictures that he said, "Mrs. Bennett, you *have* to see the bulletin board Mary Jo and I worked on! Mary Jo wrote a story about her horse and

76

I wrote a story about a Scarlet Macaw."

I wanted my mother to see the bulletin board, too, but I wasn't sure she should talk to Mrs. Whitney after what happened this morning. So I pointed at Bruno and said, "Dogs aren't allowed in school."

But Danny volunteered to hold Bruno's leash and wait outside with him. Bruno sat down as though he wasn't planning to run off, so we thought it would be OK.

Cats aren't allowed in school either, but I knew if we left Mr. Ferguson with Danny, that smart cat would figure out we wanted him to stay put and he'd walk away on purpose just to get Danny in trouble. Danny was kind of like a substitute, and Mr. Ferguson is the kind to give a sub trouble, if you know what I mean.

I could have waited outside with Danny, but I figured if my mother and Mrs. Whit-

ney were going to talk about me, I kind of
wanted to be there, too.

I promised my mother I would hold on
tight to Mr. Ferguson, so she said OK as
long as I watched him like a hawk. Besides, I thought Mrs Whitney might like
to see the cat from my bulletin board story.

Mrs. Whitney shook hands with my
mother and made a fuss over Matthew.
But she backed away from Mr. Ferguson

and started sneezing. And suddenly, before I could stop him, Mr. Ferguson jumped out of my arms and started rubbing up against Mrs. Whitney's ankles and purring.

Mrs. Whitney sneezed again and said she was allergic to cats. So I grabbed Mr. Ferguson, who was pretty mad about having to leave because he likes to bother people who are allergic to him, and I ran out of the building to where Danny was waiting with Bruno.

Fortunately, Bruno was being pretty good. Who needs two bad animals in one day? I told Mr. Ferguson I was furious because he had probably gotten me into even more trouble. I told him he was an unreasonably bad cat. I don't know if cats can actually smile, but Mr. Ferguson sure looked like he was smiling. I wouldn't want to be like Mr. Ferguson, even though

79

he usually gets his own way. Come to think of it, I wouldn't want to be like Bruno, either. Bruno is nice, but he is also wild and goofy.

My mother stayed inside for a long time talking to Mrs. Whitney. I knew they were talking about me. And I felt kind of nervous, because I didn't think they could be saying all good things.

● ● ●

I didn't get to talk to my mother right away, because Danny was still with us. But after we dropped him off, my mother told me that Mrs. Whitney said I was having some ups and downs and that she wanted to see how I would do tomorrow, after the trouble I got into today.

That made me nervous, God, because if tomorrow is not a good day, I will probably not be able to go on my trip.

I asked my mother if she thought Mrs. Whitney would hold it against me because of what Mr. Ferguson did, but my mother said no. So I guess that's all right.

● ● ●

I don't know what to do about my stars, God. I suppose I should pick off the ones from yesterday. I gave them to myself when I thought of washing the boards and when I washed them. I gave them to myself before I realized that washing the boards wasn't such a good thing to do. So maybe I should keep them. What do you think?

And I don't know about getting stars for today. I don't think people get stars for going to the principal's office, but I *was* brave about telling Mrs. Whitney it was me.

I used to think I would give myself a star

81

if I got to be T.A., but Mrs. Whitney made me T.A. before she knew about the board—and she didn't take away the badge after she knew. Maybe being T.A. is just something good that happens to you. You can't earn it by being good, and you can't lose it by being bad.

I guess I can give myself a star for having a story on the bulletin board. But I don't think I should lose a star because of Mr. Ferguson.

Love,
 Mary Jo

Friday

Dear God,

Vanessa got picked for T.A. today, and you'd think Mrs. Whitney had picked her to be a princess or something, the way Vanessa was acting. I figure that if you're a nice person, you'll be a nice T.A.—but if you're a snotty person, you'll be a snotty T.A. That's just the way it is.

I didn't mind about Vanessa being picked—everybody gets to be T.A. sometime. But I *did* mind when Vanessa picked *Julie* to be the girl T.A.'s friend. I might have known.

Julie looked at me as if to say, "What

can I do?" And I understood, because how can you turn down something like that? Besides, Julie and I just have this rule that we will pick each other. We don't have a rule that says we can't be the T.A.'s friend if somebody else picks us.

And on top of that, I didn't want to make any kind of fuss today. You know why.

I saw Vanessa get out her cute little mouse notebook, so she could write down people's names and tell on them.

This morning went all right. Except when Vanessa was handing out work sheets, she deliberately skipped the people she doesn't like.

Then somebody (not me) said, "MRS. WHITNEY!! I DIDN'T GET A PAPER!!!" Then a bunch of other kids said, "ME NEITHER!"

Mrs. Whitney told all the people who

didn't get papers to raise their hands. And Vanessa said in that phony, icky-sweet voice of hers, "I'm sorry, Mrs. Whitney, I must have skipped some people by mistake."

Ha!

I was the last one Vanessa gave a worksheet to, which meant I had to hold my hand up so long it got tired, and I had to prop it up with my other hand. Then I had to hurry and write my name and date on the paper while the rest of the class waited for me.

But Vanessa's plan backfired, because she still had to do her own paper. So the class ended up waiting for *her*.

Finally Mrs. Whitney could give us instructions. But first she said to Vanessa, "Try to be a little quicker with the papers next time, OK?"

Ha, ha for you, Vanessa, I thought.

But even when Vanessa didn't give me my paper at first, I didn't yell. And I think that's pretty good, so I will give myself a star.

● ● ●

I didn't have to sit on the wood at recess. Julie and I told Becky she could play with us. I didn't even play too wild, because I know Becky doesn't like to.

● ● ●

Everything was going fine today until we had a fire drill.

When the bell goes off we have to stop whatever we're doing and get ourselves in A-B-C order by our last names and march out the door. Vanessa's last name is Bradley, so she stands behind me. And Julie's last name is Chang, so she stands behind

Vanessa. Our classroom is on the ground floor, and I always think it would be quicker just to jump out the window, but that is against the rules. So I was good in line.

It's also against the rules to stop and get your coat even though this was a very windy day, so it was cold just standing there. Everybody started hopping on one foot and then the other and flapping and rubbing their hands on their arms to keep warm. But we still stayed in line.

Vanessa saw me rubbing my arms and hopping like everybody else, but I *wasn't* being wild at all. She had snuck out her notebook and a pencil in the pocket of her dress, and she whispered to me, "I'm going to get you in trouble, Mary Jo. I'm going to write your name down and tell Mrs. Whitney *you* were messing up in the fire drill line."

Well, I don't know exactly what happened, God. But all of a sudden the idea of Vanessa telling Mrs. Whitney something about me that wasn't true made me so mad I couldn't stand it. She probably ruined my trip when this was my last day to show I could be good, and I had been *so* good all day!

I turned around and grabbed the notebook. All I wanted to do was tear out the page that had my name on it. But Vanessa tried to grab it back, and the cover ripped in two. And then the whole notebook fell in a mud puddle.

Then Vanessa started crying real loud, because I guess the notebook was one of her favorite things. And I felt mad at her and sorry for her all at the same time.

Of course, Mrs. Whitney came running and wanted to know what happened.

Vanessa said I was messing up in line and that I had grabbed her notebook and thrown it in the puddle.

But, of course, Julie, who was standing behind us in line and who was also the girl T.A.'s friend, told the truth.

She told Mrs. Whitney I hadn't been messing up in the fire drill line and that I only grabbed the notebook because Vanessa wrote my name down and that the mud puddle was an accident.

Then Mrs. Whitney got after me for getting so upset and grabbing other people's property. Then she got after Vanessa for bringing the notebook out in the first place and for always telling on people.

Then Mrs. Whitney said that she was going to a rest home where there were green rolling hills and that she was going to make things out of clay and that none of

89

us could come visit her. That sounded to me like something my father would say when he is kidding around, so I figured Mrs. Whitney wasn't as mad as she sounded. At least I hoped not. She said she would talk to Vanessa and me more after school.

• • •

Mrs. Whitney seemed really tired when she talked to us. She said she was fed up with the fact that Vanessa and I didn't get along. She said we don't have to be friends, but we have to learn to cooperate for the good of the whole class.

She asked us one at a time if we would cooperate. And we just looked at the floor and said, "Yes," one at a time, very quietly.

Then Mrs. Whitney quickly got together some crisscrossed piles of papers for

Vanessa to take home. Vanessa's mother helps Mrs. Whitney by stapling the loose papers into packets for her. Vanessa is always bragging about that.

Some teachers came into the room then, and Mrs. Whitney shooed Vanessa and me out. So I didn't have a chance to ask Mrs. Whitney about my trip. But I figured what's the use anyway. Even if I had been perfect all week—which I wasn't exactly—

the fight with Vanessa this afternoon would have ruined things anyway.

Vanessa and I walked down the hall at the same time, but we weren't together. She walked on one side, and I walked on the other.

I am writing this on the playground. Vanessa stopped at the bathroom, and I came on out here. I thought maybe I could play a little bit to make myself feel better, but I don't really want to. And, besides, it is pretty windy.

It's probably too windy even to ride Silver Lightning one more time before I am grounded.

Vanessa just came out, so I will stop writing now.

● ● ●

Well, God, did you ever see anything like that in your whole life? I left off writing when Vanessa came out, but here's what happened after that.

Vanessa was carrying the pile of papers for her mother to staple. But you know how clumsy Vanessa is. She tripped, and the papers went flying all over the place.

I just did the first thing that popped into my head to do. I jumped up and started chasing the papers.

Vanessa could catch some of the ones closest to her, but not the ones she had to run and climb to get.

Fortunately, there's a fence around the playground, and a lot of the papers were getting caught there. But some even blew up to the monkey bars. So I climbed up after them. And when I was up that high, I could see some of the kids playing in their yards or walking along the sidewalks.

I saw Pug and Danny so I yelled in my

93

loudest loud voice, "PUG! DANNY! COME HELP!"

Curtis heard me, too, and he came running fast, which is pretty fast but not as fast as I can go.

Then I saw Julie. And then I saw Becky. So I yelled to them and to some other kids, too. And before you knew it there was a whole bunch of us running all over the playground, chasing Vanessa's papers.

Becky got the good idea of putting rocks on the papers we caught so that they wouldn't blow away again, so she and Vanessa were in charge of that.

We must have made quite a commotion, because Mrs. Whitney and some other teachers and the principal and the secretary and the janitor all rushed out to see what was going on.

And even the grown-ups chased the pa-

pers. Everybody was laughing hard, like it was a game at a party.

Finally we had all the papers we could see. Some of the papers had blown clean away from us.

Of course, the piles were all out of order, so we carried the papers back into the entrance hall and spread them out. Everybody worked to put them into the right stacks. Mr. Harley, the principal, said he didn't know when he'd ever seen such a fine example of cooperation. But I still thought it was a lot of fun.

Mrs. Whitney ran off some more papers to make up for the ones that blew away. Mrs. Miller, the secretary, lent Vanessa some rubber bands and a canvas shopping bag so that even if Vanessa dropped the papers again, they wouldn't fly away.

Then I heard Vanessa say something to

Mrs. Whitney, and I couldn't believe my ears. Vanessa told Mrs. Whitney she felt dumb for tripping and dropping the papers. I think Vanessa does a *lot* of dumb things, but I never heard *her* say that. And *then* guess what, God! Mrs. Whitney put her arm around Vanessa's shoulders and said, "Well, Vanessa, you're in good company. *I* feel really dumb for not bundling the papers up better. I should have taken the time to do that, and I didn't."

I was really surprised to hear Mrs. Whitney say that because I didn't know that grown-ups, especially teachers, ever thought they did dumb things.

But Mrs. Whitney told Vanessa, "We all make mistakes. That's why we all need a little help from our friends from time to time."

Then I *really* couldn't believe my ears,

because Vanessa told Mrs. Whitney that I was the first one to help her and that I had called all the other kids to help.

Mrs. Whitney smiled at me and put her other arm around my shoulders. And she gave both Vanessa and me a hug at the same time.

And then Mrs. Whitney thanked everyone very much for their help and told everyone to have a good weekend. But when she said that about the weekend, she looked especially at me, and she winked.

● ● ●

Guess what, God! I GET TO GO! I GET TO GO! I GET TO GO! I GET TO GO!

Mrs. Whitney called my parents just before supper. She must have been at home, and it was funny to think of my teacher calling from her house to my house. We usually just see each other at school.

Mrs. Whitney told my parents all about me helping Vanessa. And she said that really proved to her that I was trying to cooperate and get along in school. She said she thought I should be allowed to go on the trip, and my parents agreed with her. So I get to go! I get to go!

My father told me I could call my grandparents and tell them myself, but I was so excited, they couldn't understand a word I was saying.

Plus Bruno got excited because I was excited, and he started bouncing around and barking. My father said Bruno wouldn't have all that energy if he'd cleaned out the garage the way he was supposed to. Then my father told my mother that Bruno and I were two kids who shouldn't be allowed in the same *town*, let alone the same *house*.

My mother took over the phone and managed to shush Bruno. So now my grandparents know they're supposed to come get me tomorrow.

Isn't it wonderful, God? I get to go! I have to go to bed extra early tonight, which is funny because usually on Fridays I can stay up later. But Grandma and Grandpa Bennett are coming real early for me tomorrow morning. And tomorrow I will see the horse I get to ride!

I think I should give myself lots of stars. But this day turned out so good, it almost doesn't need stars.

Good night, God.

Love,
Mary Jo

Saturday

Dear God,

Sugar is the name of Mr. and Mrs. Cooper's horse. The Coopers are my grandparents' friends, and they are very nice.

I asked them if they called their horse Sugar because she likes to eat sugar, but they said no—they called her Sugar because she is so sweet and gentle.

Sugar and I liked each other right away. She is big and a kind of soft brown color. Do you know what I didn't realize until today, God? That horses are *really big* when you see them up close.

At first maybe I was just a little bit

scared of Sugar, even though I liked her. But what the Coopers said was true—she *is* a sweet horse.

Riding a horse turned out to be different than I thought it was going to be. I kept thinking it would be like the wild ponies from the movie we saw in school—that all I had to do was jump on and I could just gallop like the wind wherever I wanted to go.

But my grandfather had to get on Sugar first, and then Mr. Cooper had to lift me up so I could sit in front of my grandfather.

Sugar just walked around the field at first. Then when I got more used to her, my grandfather let her trot. And that was fast enough, I think.

Later I got to sit on Sugar all by myself, and my grandfather took Polaroid pictures. Mrs. Whitney has this time she calls

"sharing our experiences," which is mostly like Show and Tell. On Monday I'll tell about riding a horse, and I'll have the pictures to prove that I really did it.

I used to think that all horses had to have names like *Silver Lightning,* the horse name I gave my bike, but now I don't think that's the way it always has to be. At least not for every horse you meet.

I still like to think about those ponies running wild and free in the west somewhere, but I don't think Sugar has to be that way. In fact, it's a good thing Sugar is patient and calm and sweet, or I probably wouldn't have been able to ride her.

Tomorrow we are going to a little country church. I am going to ask my grandfather if he and I can ride Sugar to church.

Love,

Mary Jo

Sunday

Dear God,

My grandfather promised we could ride Sugar before we went home, but he said we couldn't ride her to church, because there was no place to put her.

I have decided that when I get home (I mean home to my own house), I will change my bike's name to Sugar—so that whenever I ride my bike, I will think of the real Sugar.

Sunday school was different, because the church didn't have enough kids to make lots of classes—so my class had all different ages. The teacher and the kids were very nice to me, but I missed Julie, Becky, Danny, Pug, and Curtis. But especially I missed Miss Jenkins.

Before I left I made my mother promise to tell Miss Jenkins where I was and that everything worked out for me to go on the trip and ride the horse. I knew Miss Jenkins would want to know how everything turned out.

Between Sunday school and church, Mrs. Cooper's friends came up to Grandma and me, and they kind of started making a fuss. I think Grandma was proud that her grandchild was getting all that attention. *I* didn't like it, because they were all talking to me like I was much younger than I am. But I didn't say anything mean, because I didn't think I should hurt their feelings or Grandma's. I'm not even going to give myself a star for that, because I think maybe

106

not hurting people's feelings is something you should just do without having to get stars for it.

It felt funny hearing a sermon from someone who wasn't Daddy. But the pastor here does the same thing Daddy does. He tells everybody to be quiet for a minute and just pray to you inside their heads.

Do you remember what I prayed about, God? I think you do, because I think you always remember what everybody says to you. I kept thinking about all the things I'm glad for. For my friends Julie and Becky. And for not being enemies with Vanessa any more even if we're not exactly friends. And I thought of Sugar, waiting in the field for me to come ride her. And very quietly I said to you, Thank you, God.

Love,

Mary Jo

107

If you enjoyed this book in The Kids from Apple Street Church series, you'll want to sneak a look at the diaries of all the kids in Miss Jenkins's Sunday school class.

1. Mary Jo Bennett
2. Danny Petrowski
3. Julie Chang
4. Pug McConnell
5. Becky Garcia
6. Curtis Anderson

You'll find these books at a Christian bookstore. Or write to Chariot Books, 850 N. Grove, Elgin, IL 60120.